eOR Rabbits

WOL

Piglet

MEET ALL THESE FRIENDS IN BUZZ BOOKS:

Thomas the Tank Engine
The Animals of Farthing Wood
Biker Mice from Mars
Fireman Sam
Joshua Jones
Rupert
Babar

First published in Great Britain in 1995 by Buzz Books
an imprint of Reed Children's Books
Michelin House, 81 Fulham Road, London SW3 6RB
and Auckland, Melbourne, Singapore and Toronto.

Copyright © 1995 Michael John Brown, Peter Janson-Smith,
Roger Hugh Vaughan Charles Morgan and Timothy Michael Robinson,
Trustees of the Pooh Properties.
Published under licence from The Walt Disney Company
Adapted from *Winnie-the-Pooh*, first published 1926 and
The House at Pooh Corner, first published 1928.
Text by A.A. Milne and drawings by E.H. Shepard
Copyright under the Berne Convention.
Adaptation of the line illustrations and colouring by Arkadia
copyright © 1995 Reed International Books Ltd.
All rights reserved
ISBN 1 855 91460 3
Printed in Italy

Winnie-the-Pooh and the Heffalump

From the stories by A.A. Milne

One fine spring day, Christopher Robin declared: "I saw a Heffalump today, Piglet."

"I think I saw one once," said Piglet, and Pooh said he had too, although he wondered what a Heffalump looked like.

Later, Pooh and Piglet were on their
way home and they came to the Six
Pine Trees.

Pooh looked round to see that
nobody else was listening and said:

"Piglet, I have decided to catch a
Heffalump!"

Pooh nodded his head several times and waited for Piglet's reply. The fact was Piglet was wishing that *he* had thought about it first.

"I shall do it," said Pooh, "by means of a trap. And it must be a Very Cunning Trap, so you will have to help me, Piglet."

Piglet felt happier now, and said, "How shall we do it?"

Pooh said, "That's just it. How?"
And then they sat down together
to think it out.

Pooh's first idea was that they should dig a Very Deep Pit, and then the Heffalump would come along and fall into it. The Heffalump might be walking along, looking up at the sky, wondering if it would rain, and so he wouldn't see the Very Deep Pit until it was too late.

Piglet thought it was a splendid idea, but what if it were already raining?

Pooh thought again and declared that, in that case, the Heffalump would be looking up at the sky wondering if it would clear up!

That settled, they now wondered where they should dig the Very Deep Pit and what they should put in it.

"Suppose," Pooh said to Piglet, "that *you* wanted to catch *me*, how would you do it?"

"Well," Piglet replied, "I should make a trap near here, and I should put a jar of honey in the trap, and you would smell it, and you would go in after it, and – "

"I would get to the jar of honey, and
I should lick around
the edges, and –"
"Never mind about
all that," said Piglet.

"Now the first thing is, what do
Heffalumps like? I should think
acorns, shouldn't you? I say,
wake up, Pooh!"

They were about to argue about
what was more 'trappy', honey or
acorns, when Piglet remembered that
if they used acorns, *he* would
have to find them, but if
they used honey, Pooh
would have to give up
some of his own.

"*I'll* dig the pit," said Piglet, "while *you* go and get the honey.

"Very well," said Pooh, and off he stumped.

As soon as Pooh got home, he went to the larder, stood on a chair and took down a very large jar from the top shelf. On the front of the jar it had HUNNY written on it.

Pooh took the honey jar along to
Piglet, who put it at the very bottom
of the Very Deep Pit. Piglet then
carefully climbed out, and they went
off home together.

"Well, goodnight, Pooh," said Piglet,
"we'll meet at six o'clock tomorrow
morning by the Six Pine Trees, to see
how many Heffalumps we've caught."

Some hours later, Pooh woke up suddenly with a sinking feeling. He had felt it before...*He was hungry.*

So he went to the larder, stood on a chair and reached up to the top shelf, and found – nothing.

"That's funny," he thought. "I know I had a jar of honey there. A full jar, full of honey right to the top, and it had HUNNY written on it."

And then he began to wander up and down, wondering where it was. And then he remembered – the Cunning Trap to catch the Heffalump.

"Bother!" Pooh said. He went back to bed, but the more he tried to sleep, the more he couldn't.

He tried counting sheep, then Heffalumps, but they were all making straight for a pot of Pooh's honey, *and eating it all!*

When he reached the five hundred and eighty-seventh Heffalump, who was licking its tusks and saying to itself, "Very good honey this. I don't know when I've tasted better," Pooh could bear it no longer.

He jumped out of bed and ran out of the house, straight to the Six Pine Trees.

In the half light, the Six Pine Trees seemed cold and lonely, and the Very Deep Pit seemed deeper than it was, and Pooh's jar of honey at the bottom was something mysterious, a shape and no more.

But as he got nearer, Pooh's nose told him that it was indeed honey, and down he climbed into the pit.

So Pooh sat down
and took a big pawful
of honey.

And then he put his tongue in, and
took a large lick, and then another
one and another one. And then to get
to the honey at the bottom of the jar,
he pushed his head right in, and
began to lick...

Piglet woke up, dreaming of Heffalumps. And then he had an idea. He would go up very quietly to the Six Pine Trees *now*, peep cautiously into the trap, and see if there was a Heffalump there.

So off he went. As he got nearer, he was sure that there was a Heffalump in the trap, because he could hear it heffalumping about like anything.

"Oh, dear, oh, dear," said Piglet. He crept to the side of the trap and looked in...

All this time, Winnie-the-Pooh had been trying to get the honey jar off his head. The more he shook it, the more it stuck. So at last, he lifted up his head, jar and all, and made a loud, roaring noise of despair...and it was at that moment that Piglet happened to look down.

"Help! Help!" he cried, and scampered as fast as he could to Christopher Robin's house.

"Whatever is the matter, Piglet?" said Christopher Robin.

"A Heffalump...It had the biggest head you ever saw – like – like a jar!"

"Well," said Christopher Robin. "Let's go and look at it." So off they went and soon they came to the Very Deep Pit.

Suddenly, Christopher Robin began to laugh...and he laughed and he laughed. And while he was still laughing – *Crash* went the Heffalump's head against a tree root. *Smash* went the jar, and out came Pooh!

"Oh, Pooh Bear!" said Christopher
Robin. "How I do love you!"
"So do I," said Pooh.

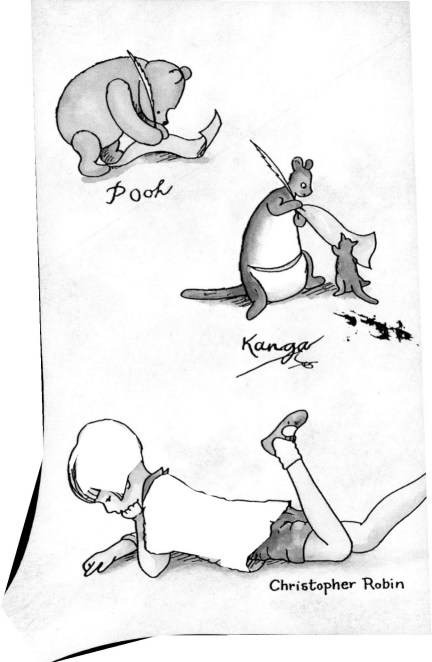

Pooh

Kanga

Christopher Robin